WINNIE~THE~POOH

The Little Book of Wisdom

Wise words from the **Best Bear** in All the World

A. A. MILNE
with decorations by **E. H. SHEPARD**

Farshore

First published in Great Britain 1999 by Egmont UK Limited
This edition published in Great Britain 2020 by Farshore
An imprint of HarperCollins*Publishers*
1 London Bridge Street, London SE1 9GF
www.farshore.co.uk

HarperCollins*Publishers*
1st Floor, Watermarque Building, Ringsend Road, Dublin 4, Ireland

Winnie-the-Pooh's Little Book of Wisdom adapted from *Winnie-the-Pooh* first published 1926
and *The House at Pooh Corner* first published 1928
Text by A.A.Milne copyright © Trustees of the Pooh Properties
Line illustrations copyright © E.H.Shepard
Colouring of the illustrations copyright © 1970-1974 E.H.Shepard and HarperCollins*Publishers*
Colouring of the line illustrations by Mark Burgess copyright © 1989 HarperCollins*Publishers*

ISBN 978 1 4052 9759 2
Printed in China.
002

'It isn't Brain,' said Pooh humbly,
'because You Know Why;
but it comes to me sometimes.'

Before You Begin

Pooh is a Bear of Very Little Brain who can't always
think of the right words to say, but even so has said
some very wise words and thought some very interesting
thoughts, which he would like to share with you.
Poetry and Hums and little Words of Wisdom aren't
things which Pooh gets, they are things which get him.
All he can do is go where they can find him.
So, reader go where they can find you, too and dip your
paws into this little collection of Wisdom from an
Astute and Helpful Bear, The Best Bear in
All the World, Winnie-the-Pooh.

Personal Thoughts

When you are a Bear of very Little Brain, and you Think of Things, you sometimes find that a Thing which seemed very Thingish inside you is quite different when it gets out in the open and has other people looking at it.

Set Priorities

*Nearly eleven o'clock is time for
a little smackerel of something.*

Check Your Store Cupboard

It's sort of comforting to know if you have fourteen pots of honey left, or fifteen, as the case may be.

Have a Friendly Day

When you've been walking in the wind for miles, and you suddenly go into somebody's house, and he says, 'Hallo, Pooh, you're just in time for a little smackerel of something,' and you are, then it's what I call a Friendly Day.

Take Time to Relax

What I like doing best is Nothing. It's when people call out at you just as you're going off to do it, 'What are you going to do?' and you say 'Oh Nothing,' and then you go and do it. Doing Nothing means just going along, listening to all the things you can't hear, and not bothering.

Control Your Stress Levels

*To seem quite at ease, hum tiddely-pom
once or twice in a what-shall-we-do-now
kind of way.*

A Little Caution

When you go after honey with a balloon, the great thing is not to let the bees know you're coming.

A Matter of Taste

The wrong sort of bees would make the wrong sort of honey.

Keep Busy

It's just the day for doing things.

Enjoy Yourself

What I like best in the whole world is Me and Piglet going to see You, and You saying 'What about a little something?' and Me saying, 'Well, I shouldn't mind a little something, should you, Piglet,' and it being a hummy sort of day outside, and birds singing.

Assess Your Surroundings

When your house doesn't look like a house and looks like a tree that has been blown down, it is time you tried to find another one.

Insight

*It's best to know what you are looking for
before you look for it.*

Accept Yourself

'Pooh,' said Rabbit kindly, 'you haven't any brain.'
'I know,' said Pooh humbly.

Improve Your Brain Power

How wonderful to have a Real Brain which could tell you things.

Self Knowledge

Pooh hasn't much Brain, but he never comes to any harm. He does silly things and they turn out right.

You Can't Be Good at Everything

When you are a Bear of Very Little Brain
you're never much good at riddles.

Management Skills

A Very Clever Brain could catch a Heffalump if he knew the right way to go about it.

Keeping Trim

A bear, however hard he tries,
Grows tubby without exercise.

Why You Can't

It all comes of liking honey so much.

Companionship

It isn't much good having anything exciting,
if you can't share it with somebody.

It's so much more friendly with two.

Admire Someone

You can't help respecting anybody who can spell
TUESDAY.

Self Appreciation

'What sort of stories does he like?'
'About himself. Because he's that sort of Bear.'

The Best Bear in all the World.

Time Management

'*They always take longer than you think.*' said Rabbit.
'*How long do you think they'll take?*' asked Roo.

Take the Initiative

Like Rabbit, never let things come to you,
always go out and fetch them.

Be Prepared

Brush the honey off your nose,
spruce yourself up so as to look
Ready for Anything.

Sociability

*A good reason for going to see
everybody is because it's Thursday.*

Whenever You Feel Afraid

*To show you haven't been frightened jump up and
down once or twice in an exercising sort of way.*

Make a Brave Gesture

Just hum to yourself as if you are
waiting for something.

Be Careful!

You can never tell with bees, you can never tell with paw-marks, and you can never tell with Heffalumps.

Don't Worry

When you get a sinking feeling, don't worry,
it's probably because you're hungry.

Spare Time

While you wonder what to do,
sit down and sing a song.

Punctuality

*Don't be late for whatever
you want to be in time for.*

Try a Little Spontaneity

Do a good thing
without thinking about it.

If at First You Don't Succeed

If the string breaks, try another piece of string.

Gastronomic Disappointment

*A Very Nearly tea is one you
forget about afterwards.*

Always Ask

Being a Faithful Knight might mean you just go on being faithful without being told things.

Look on the Bright Side

Everybody is all right really.
That's what I think.

Manners

Always say Goodbye-and-
thank-you-for-a-nice-time.

Love Your Neighbour as Yourself

'Oh Bear!' said Christopher Robin.
'How I do love you!'
'So do I,' said Pooh.

Look Out!

An Ambush is a sort of surprise.
So is a gorse-bush sometimes.

Listening Skills

There are twelve pots of honey in my cupboard and they've been calling me for hours. I couldn't hear them properly before because Rabbit would keep talking, but if nobody says anything except those twelve pots, then I shall know where they're coming from.

Be Caring

A little Consideration, a little Thought for Others, makes all the difference.